Puffin Books

A Wee Walk

Jock, the Scottish terrier, and Old Mac are best friends. Every day, they go for a walk down the street. Old Mac does his shopping and Jock picks up and answers his 'wee-mails'. Life couldn't be better.

From a wooden seat Jock finds out he is going to be a father. And from the peppercorn tree he learns that the *Every Dog Has Its Day Party* is this Saturday!

But things don't always go according to plan, and there are some surprises in store for Jock and Old Mac.

A cheeky and touching story from the one and only Margaret Clark.

Also by Margaret Clark

The Chickabees
Hot and Spicy
Stars
Sugar, Sugar
Far from Phoneys
Brush With Fame
Bewitched

The Mango Street Series
Weird Warren
Butterfingers
Wally the Whiz Kid
Britt the Boss
Wacky Mac
Copycat
Millie the Moaner
Bold As Brass

Other titles
Snap!
Crackle!
Pop!
S.N.A.G.
Board Shorts
Boxer Shorts
Dirty Shorts
Footy Shorts
Holey Shorts
Stinky Shorts
Pugwall
Pugwall's Summer
Love on the Net
Rave On

40696

A Wee Walk

Margaret Clark

illustrated by
Craig Smith

Puffin Books

Puffin Books
Penguin Books Australia Ltd
487 Maroondah Highway, PO Box 257
Ringwood, Victoria 3134, Australia
Penguin Books Ltd
Harmondsworth, Middlesex, England
Penguin Putnam Inc.
375 Hudson Street, New York, New York 10014, USA
Penguin Books Canada Limited
10 Alcorn Avenue, Toronto, Ontario, Canada M4V 3B2
Penguin Books (NZ) Ltd
Cnr Rosedale and Airborne Roads, Albany, Auckland, New Zealand
Penguin Books (South Africa) (Pty) Ltd
5 Watkins Street, Denver Ext 4, 2094, South Africa
Penguin Books India (P) Ltd
11, Community Centre, Panchsheel Park, New Delhi 110 017, India

First published by Penguin Books Australia, 2001

1 3 5 7 9 10 8 6 4 2

Designed by Susannah Low, Penguin Design Studio
Typeset in New Century Schoolbook 16/20
by Post Pre-press Group, Brisbane, Queensland
Made and printed in Australia by Australian Print Group,
Maryborough, Victoria

National Library of Australia
Cataloguing-in-Publication data:

Clark, M. D. (Margaret Dianne), 1943-
A wee walk
ISBN 0 14 131268 8

Dogs Juvenile fiction. I. Smith, Craig, 1955- II. Title

A823.3

To
Lisa Adderly,
and Ben and Rebecca Norman,
who all like Scottie dogs called Jock.
To Dorsey and Daisy, who live with
Miranda on the corner.
And to my dad who
loved walking Honey and Kelly.

Chapter One

'Come on, Jock. Let's go for our walk,' said Old Mr Mac. 'It's a lovely sunny day.'

Old Mr Mac got his coat and his tartan cap from the hook on the porch wall, and put them on.

Jock waited patiently while Old Mr Mac snapped the dog-leash clip onto his tartan collar.

Then Old Mr Mac picked up his walking stick. And off they went together, slowly down the path.

Jock stopped to sniff near the gatepost, as he always did.

There was a new message. 'Jock. Meet you in the park at ten. Boofa.'

Jock left his message. 'I can't, Boofa. I'm really busy today with Old Mr Mac. We are going to the shops and the beach. We have lots of things to see and lots of things to do.'

Chapter Two

Old Mr Mac and Jock
walked down the street.

Jock stopped to check out
the telephone pole.

There were two messages.

'Hi, Jock. I'm
going to the vet
today. Oscar.'

And, 'This is
Brutus. Get off
my turf or else!'

Jock left two short messages. 'Good luck with the vet.' And 'Bad luck, I'm staying. So get off *my* turf!'

They walked to the corner, past a fat black cat lazing in the sun.

Jock could read the message just by looking at her. It said, 'Come near me and I'll scratch your nose!'

So Jock put *his* nose up in the air and walked straight past.

He didn't need any trouble with a fat, black cat.

Or a scratch on the nose!

He needed to keep his nose clean and shiny for other things, like sniffing and getting messages.

Chapter Three

Old Mr Mac and Jock crossed the road at the traffic lights.

Jock checked the new spring grass that was growing at the base of a wooden seat on the edge of the footpath.

There was a new message. It said, 'Jock. I'm having pups. Love, Mitzi.'

He sniffed it again,
just to make sure.

Yes. There was no mistake! He, Jock
MacTavish, the Scottie dog, was going
to be a father!

Mitzi was a very attractive white Maltese terrier.

Maybe the pups would be half black, like him, and half white, like Mitzi.

They would be a new breed of dog!

Black and White Whiskeries.

Or maybe they would be Malteasers.

Jock tried to tell Old Mr Mac, but he was too busy to listen right at that moment. Jock was annoyed. He yapped some more.

'Stop yapping and hurry up, Jock,' said Old Mr Mac. 'We've got lots of things to see and lots of things to do.'

Chapter Four

They walked along a bit
further. Jock knew what would
happen next. He'd lived with
Old Mr Mac for ten years.

Old Mr Mac stopped. He tied
Jock's leash to the bike rack,
while he went into the shop
to buy a newspaper.

Jock sniffed the bottom of the
bike rack. There were two
messages for him.

'Congratulations,
new dad. From Fido.'

'I thought you
loved *me*. Buffy!'

No way! Buffy was a bossy brown
Bull Terrier with bad breath.

Jock did *not* love Buffy. He loved
Mitzi!

Old Mr Mac returned with his rolled up paper under his arm, just as Jock was getting ready to leave two quick messages.

'Thanks, Fido.' Then . . .

'Hurry up, Jock,' interrupted Old Mr Mac. 'We have lots of things to see and lots of things to do.'

'Wait!' yapped Jock. 'I need more time!'

But Old Mr Mac tugged the lead.

Jock got confused.

'Thanks, Buffy.' Oops. Wrong message.

Now he was in big trouble.

Chapter Five

Old Mr Mac and Jock walked past the house where two Airedales called Hairy and Mary lived.

Old Mr Mac called them *Hairdales* because they were so shaggy-baggy. They had curly brown fur and long legs. Whenever Old Mr Mac and Jock strolled past, they always stopped to talk to Hairy and Mary.

'I like them because they have square heads a bit like you, Jock,' Old Mr Mac always said, as he patted Hairy and Mary. 'But I like your short, straight black fur and your short, stumpy legs much better!'

Jock looked through the gate. Why weren't Hairy and Mary on the porch like they usually were at this time of the day?

What had happened to them?

'I wonder where those two Hairdales are?' said Old Mr Mac. 'Maybe they've gone to get a haircut.' He chuckled at his little joke.

Jock tried to find out where Hairy and Mary had gone.

Maybe they'd left a message.

He sniffed at the fence. But there were no new messages.

So he left a quick one. 'I'm going to be a father. From Jock.'

Chapter Six

Old Mr Mac and Jock arrived at the steps that lead down to the beach.

Jock pulled back on the leash and planted his four feet firmly. He wanted to stop. There were sure to be messages near the seat.

'Tired, wee Jock?' said Old Mr Mac. 'Have a rest, then.'

He looped the leash over a slat on the seat.

Then he sat down on the seat to read his paper, as he always did.

Jock sniffed around the base of the seat for his messages.

'Warning. Fleas in grass.
Do not roll.'

'Mad and bad dog called Rex will bite on sight.'

'Paw danger. Broken glass near statue.'

Old Mr Mac was reading out loud from the paper, as he always did.

'There's a flea plague. Hmm. I must buy you a new flea collar, wee Jock.

'Problem with stray dogs. Hmm. People should look after their dogs.

'Boys smash bottles at beach. Hmm. They should be made to clean up the mess.

'I don't know what the world's coming to, I really don't.'

But Jock was too busy to worry about the rest of the world.

He was leaving, 'Message received. Over and out.'

Chapter Seven

Old Mr Mac and Jock walked along the boardwalk.

There weren't any boards because it was made of concrete. Sometimes there were people on rollerblades and people on skateboards.

'That must be why it's called a boardwalk,' Jock thought, as he trotted along beside Old Mr Mac.

Everyone said, 'Good morning' to them. Jock thought they were lucky. Old Mr Mac said he was never lonely even though he lived by himself. And, as he said, he wasn't alone because he had his best friend, Jock.

They stopped at the water fountain.

Old Mr Mac got out his plastic cup and had a little drink of water.

Jock had a big drink from the special bowl on the ground marked, DOGS ONLY.

'Come on, Jock,' said Old Mr Mac. 'We have lots of things to see and lots of things to do.'

And they kept walking.

At the base of the sign that said,
DOGS MUST BE ON A LEASH AT
ALL TIMES there was a message. It
was from Fifi, the French poodle.

It said, 'Hi, Jock. I'm going to France
on Monday. Fifi.'

Jock left a message. 'I'm going to be a
father. Jock.'

Chapter Eight

Old Mr Mac and Jock walked to the Internet cafe.

'Maybe Morag has sent me an email,' said Old Mr Mac, as he went inside.

Morag was Old Mr Mac's daughter. She lived on the other side of town.

Jock checked his wee-mails near
the door.

'Gone to Darwin.
Love, Dad.'

'Gone to Melbourne.
Love, Mum.'

'Gone to Wagga.
Love, Aunt
Waggie.'

Everyone was on holidays!
Except wee Fiona, Jock's sister.

Jock left three short wee-mails
of his own. The first one said, 'I
haven't got time for a holiday. Love,
Jock.' The second one said, 'I'm very,
very busy walking with Old Mr Mac.
Love, Jock.' And the third said, 'I'm
going to be a father! Love, Jock.'

Chapter Nine

Old Mr Mac and Jock walked past
the butcher's.

Jock checked the drainpipe
for his messages.

But the butcher had hosed the gutter
and all the messages had gone down
the drain.

Jock left a message anyway.
'Big wash-out. Please repeat all
messages. From Jock.'

The butcher came out and gave Jock a large, juicy bone.

Old Mr Mac carried his newspaper and Jock carried his bone.

'We're going to the cake shop now, Jock,' said Old Mr Mac.

Jock trotted along, looking neither right nor left but straight ahead.

He was in a hurry to get home now.

He wanted to bury the bone in his back garden, where it would be safe.

But then Old Mr Mac and Jock met a rough, tough-looking dog.

The dog stared at Jock's bone and growled.

'Clear off,' said Old Mr Mac to the rough, tough dog.

He always stuck up for Jock. After all, they were a team!

He waved his walking stick at it.

The rough, tough dog got a fright. It put its tail between its legs and slunk away.

Jock left it a message on a fence. 'Find your own bone!'

Chapter Ten

Then Old Mr Mac and Jock walked to the cake shop.

'I think we'd better buy a Dundee cake, Jock,' said Old Mr Mac. 'We could get a visitor or two. And the thing they would like best for afternoon tea would be a Dundee cake, don't you think?'

'Woof,' mumbled Jock, through a mouthful of bone.

Just then, Mr Sims came round the corner. He was Mitzi's owner.

But Mitzi wasn't with him.

Jock whined anxiously.

'Mrs Sims has taken Mitzi to the vet for her pregnancy check-up. She's going to have puppies in about a month's time,' Mr Sims said to Old Mr Mac.

Jock wagged his tail like mad. He wanted to give a big smile too, only then he would have to drop the bone. It was too risky.

'Hmm,' said Old Mr Mac. 'Jock's keen on Mitzi. Very keen. I think he might be the father. Don't you?'

'Time will tell,' said Mr Sims with a smile.

But then he frowned as he stared at his wet shoe.

'Jock!' said Old Mr Mac in a very cross voice.

'It's okay. He probably got a bit excited,' said Mr Sims with a shrug.

Jock had left a wee message for Mitzi on Mr Sims's shoe.

It said,

'I love you forever.
From Jock.'

Old Mr Mac tied Jock to a post
outside the cake shop while he went
in to buy the Dundee cake.

Jock loved the currants best of all.
And the sugary, buttery flavour was
nearly better than a juicy bone. But
not quite!

Jock had a bit of a sniff.

There were no messages for him.

He left a short message anyway.
'Jock was here.'

'Come on, Jock,' said Old Mr Mac
when he came out of the shop.
'We're going home.'

Old Mr Mac didn't hurry. He walked slowly. It had been a long walk today.

Jock stopped to check underneath the big peppercorn tree.

Old Mr Mac stopped, too. He opened the brown paper bag to have a peek at the Dundee cake.

Jock wondered if it was an excuse
for Old Mr Mac to have a rest.
He seemed to be getting tired lately.

Jock knew that there were not
many more things to see and do.

They were nearly home.

'Come on, Jock. Nearly there!' said
Old Mr Mac, tugging on the leash.

Jock was glad that they were nearly
home because the bone was getting
heavier and heavier!

Chapter Eleven

Old Mr Mac and Jock walked past the police station.

Jock checked for messages.

'Busy catching some robbers. Back at ten a.m. From Sam.'

Sam was the police dog. He was trained to do all sorts of interesting jobs.

Jock left a quick 'Hi from Jock,' and kept walking.

Then he sniffed at the grass under the wattle tree.

There were two messages.

One was from Madonna, the German Shepherd. She was quite a gossip and liked to leave long messages.

It said,'To whom It May Concern.

'This is to let you know that
Hairy and Mary, the two prize
Airedales who live in the corner
house, have gone to a Dog Show
in the city to compete in the
world-famous Airedale section.
They won't be back for three
days. We all wish them every
success and hope that one of
them, or both of them, will win
their sections and get the silver
cup for first prize.'

It certainly was a long message.

But then Madonna was a big dog
with big wee-capacity. And not a
wee Scottie like Jock, with wee
wee-capacity!

'I hope Hairy and Mary both win their Dog Show sections,' thought Jock. 'They might show me their winners' cups.'

Chapter Twelve

Jock had a good long sniff at the second message.

It was shorter. But exciting.

It said, 'This is an invitation to the annual *Every Dog Has Its Day Party* on Saturday at the park, six p.m. sharp. BYO bones and owners. RSVPee now. Are you coming? Yes or no. From Bozo the Boxer.'

Bozo belonged to the butcher. That's how he knew about the party before anyone else.

Once a year Bruno the butcher held a big barbecue.

He provided the meat.

Everyone else brought the salads and other food.

And their dogs.

There would be sausages and
hamburgers and chops and
steaks sizzling on the barbecue
for all the owners.

They thought it was *their* annual
get-together.

But all the dogs knew differently.

A party!

Jock loved the annual owner-and-dog party, even though some of the bossy dogs, like Buffy, wanted to bite and fight.

He'd be able to see Mitzi. And all his other friends.

And maybe he and Mitzi could make the big announcement about their puppies!

One of the dog owners always took
along a bat and ball to play cricket.

Jock loved to chase the ball on his
short, stumpy legs. But he ran out of
puff quickly nowadays. He was
getting older, and he got tired easily
if he ran too much.

Still, it would be good to have a party in the park.

Old Mr Mac stopped to look at the Dundee cake again.

'Not as many currants today,' he said.

Jock wondered if he was really counting currants or having a rest.

Old Mr Mac closed the paper bag and tugged on the leash.

Then he sighed when he saw Jock get ready to RSVPee.

'I think you must have used up every drop in the world, wee Jock.'

But Jock managed a very, *very* short message to answer his party invitation.

It said, 'Yes. Love, Jock.'

Chapter Thirteen

It was now Friday, the day before the party.

Jock couldn't wait to see Mitzi. He hoped she was getting plenty of vitamins. But then Mr and Mrs Sims would make sure she did. He had to stop *worrying*!

Old Mr Mac and Jock were going for a walk.

'It's only a wee walk today, Jock, because there's a right nip in the air,' said Old Mr Mac.

Jock knew that a person or a dog wasn't actually going to nip them.

Old Mr Mac meant that the weather had turned chilly, and it was so cold that it nipped at his nose.

It nipped at Jock's nose, too. He sniffed very carefully at the frosty grass.

Old Mr Mac was in a hurry. They only went to the paper shop and the cake shop for another Dundee cake.

They didn't go to the beach. Or the park. In fact, they only went round the block and there wasn't much time for messages.

Jock felt a bit stressed because they were in such a hurry.

He only had three wee moments of peace and quiet to himself because Old Mr Mac was shivering.

Even though he had buttoned his coat right up to his chin and was wearing his tartan scarf, as well as his tartan cap, he was still feeling cold.

'That wind goes right through my bones, Jock,' Old Mr Mac said, as they turned into the gate and walked up the path. 'Right through my bones.'

'Woof,' said Jock. He tried to tell
Old Mr Mac that the wind
wouldn't go right through his
bones if he buried them in the
garden.

But Old Mr Mac never listened.
He kept his bones in the fridge.

Jock couldn't quite work out how
the wind got into the fridge when
they went for a walk.

It was weird!

Chapter Fourteen

Old Mr Mac had bought the Dundee cake for tomorrow's *Every Dog Has Its Day Party*.

He carefully put it in a clean cake tin, with a tight round lid so it would stay nice and fresh.

Old Mr Mac got out the step ladder to put the tin on a high shelf in the pantry.

'That's so I'm not tempted to eat a slice or two before the party, Jock,' he said.

Jock had a big shin-bone buried in the garden, ready to dig up and take to the party.

Old Mr Mac climbed up the steps, balancing the cake tin.

But then something awful happened.

Old Mr Mac slipped.

He came tumbling down the steps and landed with a thump on the floor.

The cake tin went rolling and rolling across the floorboards.

'Woof?' asked Jock, licking Old Mr Mac's face anxiously. 'Woof?'

But Old Mr Mac didn't say anything.

He looked very pale. And he was very still.

Jock put back his head and howled. And howled.

'Wake up, Old Mr Mac. Wake up!'

But Old Mr Mac didn't stir.

What was Jock going to do?

Chapter Fifteen

Jock ran to the front door.

He scratched at it with his stubby front legs. He whined and whined.

But nobody heard him.

He jumped on the sofa and looked out the window.

A woman with two small children was walking past.

Jock barked and barked and scratched his paws on the glass.

'Hello, wee Jock,' the woman called.

The children smiled and waved at him.

'Woof, woof, woof,' yelped Jock desperately. But they kept walking straight past.

More people walked past. Then Jock saw some children going for a walk with their teacher.

'Hello, Jock,' they called, waving at him.

'Woof, woof, woof!' Jock yowled frantically.

But they kept on walking.

What should he do now?

Chapter Sixteen

Jock went running back to Old Mr Mac and licked his face.

'Wake up, wake up!' he woofed.

But Old Mr Mac just lay there, and he didn't move at all.

His face was pale and he had a big bump coming up on the side of his forehead.

Jock sat on his haunches and thought hard.

It was nearly ten. Sam, the police dog, would be back soon.

Jock quickly ran out through his doggie door and down to the police station.

He left an urgent message
for Sam.

'Old Mr Mac had a bad
accident at home. Bring
help. Jock!'

He tried barking as
well, but no-one came.

He couldn't waste time.
He had to get back to
Old Mr Mac!

Chapter Seventeen

At last a policeman came and banged on the front door.

Sam the police dog was with him.

Jock ran out through his doggie door at the back, and barked and barked.

'I dragged him here,' woofed Sam.

Jock whined and pawed at the
policeman's leg.

'Is something wrong with Old Mr
Mac?' asked the policeman.

'Woof. Woof!'

The front door was locked and the policeman couldn't crawl through the doggie door. Neither could Sam.

The policeman slid the window open and climbed inside. Sam stayed outside, keeping guard.

As soon as the policeman saw Old Mr Mac on the floor he phoned for an ambulance.

Jock wouldn't leave Old Mr Mac's side. He growled when the policeman tried to clip on his leash.

The ambulance arrived in no time.

'Faithful old dog,' said Bob, the ambulance man. 'Can't we take him with us?'

They let Jock come along for the ride. But he had to sit on the floor, so that no-one could see him.

The policeman followed the ambulance
in his police car. From the hospital
the policeman phoned Old Mr Mac's
daughter, Morag, to let her know
what had happened.

Morag arrived in a big rush. By now
Old Mr Mac was wide awake and
wanting to know where Jock was.

'He's tied up outside,' said Morag.
'But don't worry, Dad. I'll take him
home with me.'

So Morag led Jock to her car.

'Old Mr Mac's going to be all right,'
said Morag to Jock. He looked very
sad sitting on the front seat of her
car.

'Cheer up, Jock. You are a very good
and brave dog. I know that
somehow you sent a message to
Sam the police dog. Maybe you can
show me how you did it.'

Jock thought about this. Then he
decided that he wouldn't. He didn't
want to get put out of the car! So
he just gave a tired woof.

'I'll look after you until my dad is better. Okay? It will be like a little holiday for you.'

Jock sighed. He really didn't need a little holiday. Not right now.

He was going to be a father. And he had to find out if Mitzi was feeling well, or if she needed any special food. He had some lovely bones ripening in the garden for her.

He also wanted to know if Hairy and Mary had won the Airedale Championships.

He had to collect his messages. He had to *leave* his messages.

And he was supposed to go to the annual *Every Dog Has Its Day Party*, and take Old Mr Mac with him.

But Old Mr Mac was in hospital, and things had changed.

Morag lived in another part of the city. And Jock couldn't even leave a message to tell the others where he was going.

But Jock kept his sad thoughts to himself and licked Morag's hand. He was grateful to have a home to go to. He did not want to be put in a dog-minding place, like Buffy sometimes was.

Morag lived alone but she had a canary called Tweetie for company.

Tweetie didn't mind Jock coming to stay. In fact, she even sang a few songs to cheer him up!

But, that night, as he lay curled up on a blanket in Morag's laundry, Jock was worried.

He belonged to Old Mr Mac and Old Mr Mac belonged to him. They had never been apart before, not even for a day.

What if Old Mr Mac was fretting for him?

Chapter Eighteen

Morag was up early, although she had the day off work.

She put on her coat and her tartan scarf. She clipped the dog leash onto Jock's collar, then picked up her basket.

'Come on, Jock, let's go for our walk,' she said. 'We have to go to the shops. We've got lots of things to do.'

Jock was fretting about the party, which was going to be later that day. He just *had* to see Mitzi! He didn't want to go for a walk.

He pulled back. But Morag pulled harder.

Jock sighed. Maybe he could escape
later and get himself to the party.
The big problem was that he didn't
know this part of town!

They walked down the path and
through the front gate.

Jock stopped to sniff at a tree for any
general messages, but Morag tugged
on the leash.

'We're in a hurry, Jock,' she said. 'We have lots of things to do.'

'Woof,' said Jock, annoyed at not being able to leave a message for whoever was passing by.

Old Mr Mac always said there were lots of things to see and lots of things to do, too. But Morag didn't seem to have time to look at *anything*.

Jock managed to leave two quick messages as they went down the street. One was on a fence and the other on a pole. Both messages said, 'Hi, I'm Jock and I'm just visiting.'

Morag tied Jock to a post while she went into the butcher's.

There were lots of messages around
the post, but none were for him. He
was about to leave one. But a woman
who was walking past glared at him
and said, 'How disgusting!'

Poor Jock was upset. He never left
disgusting messages. Ever.

What sort of dog did she think he was?

A little girl bent to pat him. Jock wagged his tail, but the man with the little girl pulled her away.

'Don't touch that dog. It's probably got fleas,' he said sharply.

Fleas? Jock looked huffy. He didn't have fleas! He decided to leave a message.

'Jock is flealess. Pass it on!'

Morag came hurrying out and grabbed his leash.

'Can you hang on, Jock?' she said. 'This is a restricted area. Can't you see the notice which says, "Be responsible for your dog."? I'm taking you to the park!'

Restricted area? Jock looked around. There was plenty of space.

And Jock MacTavish was a very responsible dog!

He never left messes on the footpath.
He never tried to bite anyone. He
didn't bark at people, either.

He was a user-friendly dog, but
this was NOT a dog-friendly
neighbourhood.

Chapter Nineteen

Morag called into the fruit shop, the chemist and the corner store. And then they walked briskly to the park.

'This basket's getting heavy,' she grumbled, putting it down on the path so that she could have a rest.

'Woof,' said Jock politely. If there was a bone in the basket he could carry it for her. He put his nose in the basket and had a sniff. He could smell meat, but was it a bone?

Before he could check it out
thoroughly, Morag picked up the
basket and pulled on his leash.

'Come on, Jock. We've still got lots of
things to do!'

She started hurrying along the path
again and didn't give him a chance to
explore the contents of her basket.

'Usually I go to the big supermarket in my car,' she said to Jock. 'But you need a walk, so I thought I'd kill two birds with one stone.'

Jock was horrified. He stopped so suddenly that Morag had to yank hard on the leash to get him going again.

Kill two birds? With a stone?

Jock looked around. He couldn't see any stones. Maybe they were in Morag's basket. Maybe that was why it was so heavy. And he couldn't see any birds. What did she mean?

But when they got to the park there were lots of birds there, big and small. They were being fed breadcrumbs by people sitting on the benches.

As soon as Morag let Jock off his leash, he went dashing over to them, barking his head off.

'Fly away.
    Stones coming.
Fly away. Stones coming!'

The birds all flew away in a big hurry, and the people were *not* pleased.

'Control your dog, lady,' said a man.

'Yes. He should be on a leash if he can't behave himself,' said a woman.

And to make matters worse, two children started to cry because the birds had flown away.

'You are a naughty dog, Jock,' said Morag, and she clipped on his leash. 'You can walk next to me and behave yourself. We're going straight back home!'

Poor Jock hung his head and put his tail between his legs.

This was not a good day!

Chapter Twenty

At last Old Mr Mac was coming home!

It was Sunday. It seemed like weeks since Old Mr Mac had been taken to hospital, but it was really only two days.

Morag drove to the hospital to pick him up.

'Stay there while I get my dad,' she said to Jock.

Jock didn't think this was a good time to tell her that dogs weren't supposed to be left alone in cars. But at least it was a cool day and she'd left the windows rolled down.

He stood up on the back seat as far
as the seat belt would allow and
gazed out the window. There was a
thick clump of bushes near the car.

There were probably messages galore
there!

He watched and watched for Morag
to come back with Old Mr Mac, but
she didn't. Morag was a kind person,
but she didn't understand dogs at all.

And she certainly didn't know how
Jock thought and felt. Not like his
beloved Old Mr Mac, who knew
Jock's every thought.

Finally, Jock gave up looking out the
window. He curled up in a small
black ball on the seat and went to
sleep.

Thump! Jock woke with a jump. The car door was opening! And – it was Old Mr Mac.

He was wearing his coat and tartan cap and leaning on his walking stick. How had those things got to the hospital?

Never mind.

Jock yelped and wiggled with joy as Old Mr Mac patted and cuddled him. Then Old Mr Mac took off Jock's seat belt, picked him up, and cuddled him some more while he got in the front seat.

'You're such a smart dog, Jock,' said

Old Mr Mac as he shut the door.

Jock looked at Morag then settled
onto his owner's lap.

Morag started the engine and smiled
at Jock.

They were going home!

Chapter Twenty-One

Jock looked out the window as they drove.

Soon it would be lunch time. The sun was shining and it was turning into a fine, warm day.

'Jock has been cooped up for too long,' said Morag. 'I think he needs a quick run in the park.'

So she drove down the street that led to the park and pulled up in a parking place.

There weren't many spaces. The car park was full. And there seemed to be lots of people.

When they saw Morag's car, the people gave a great cheer and started running across the grass.

Jock gave a wuffle of excitement. He could see Mitzi. And Bozo. And Hairy and Mary. And Fifi. And Fido. And Buffy. In fact, all his friends were running in circles, yelping their heads off.

'The date of the annual get-together was changed, Dad,' smiled Morag.

'That's right,' said Bruno the butcher. 'It wasn't a proper get-together without Old Mr Mac and wee Jock.'

Old Mr Mac and Jock walked slowly across to the barbecue area. Jock was worried that Old Mr Mac might fall over, but he seemed okay.

There was a big banner that said, 'Welcome Home, Old Mr Mac and Jock.'

'Where is Jock?' asked Morag.

Jock had rubbed noses with Mitzi and his friends. And now he was busy leaving an important message.

'To whom it may concern. Jock is here to stay and you'd better believe it.'

But then there was a more important message to announce. He and Mitzi did it together.

'We are going to have some puppies. Very soon!'